A Note from the Author

The idea for Luck came from a story in a newspaper. It was a true story about a man who had been very unlucky again and again – and then he won the Lottery.

When I wrote the book, I turned this man into Greg. He's a good friend of Dale's mum. Dale is a boy who feels unlucky, too. But as Greg says, "Nobody can be unlucky all the time." Is this true for Dale? Read on to find out!

To anyone having a tough time – it can only get better

Luck

by

Alison Prince

Illustrated by Patrick Morgan

Published in 2004 in Great Britain by
Barrington Stoke Ltd, Sandeman House, Trunk's Close,
55 High Street, Edinburgh EH1 1SR

ISBN 1-842991-99-X

Printed in Great Britain by Bell & Bain Ltd

Barrington Stoke gratefully acknowledges support from the
Scottish Arts Council towards the publication of the
gr8reads series

Scottish
Arts Council
LOTTERY FUNDED

Contents

Chapter 1
Mum

My mum is a slag.

That's what I used to think. She had a lot of boyfriends – she got them off the Internet most of the time. They were all the same – smart guys who wanted some fun. I didn't like them, and they didn't like me. None of them stayed long.

Mum said she wanted a nice man who'd look after her. That's why she kept trying new ones. My dad got killed in a car crash. It was 10 years ago, when I'd just started school. I liked my dad.

I was 15 and I wanted a girlfriend. Mum had all these boyfriends but I didn't have a girlfriend. I felt bad about it. I kept trying, but I had no luck. Girls didn't like me.

I liked Karen, at my school. I liked seeing her play netball – she had red hair and fantastic legs.

We met in the chippie once and I got her a burger, but she went off with an older guy who sold cars.

I liked Sharon, too. She was a bit fat, but all the boys said she was sexy. I got her a Coke and asked her for a date, but she said I was a prat.

Why did she say that? I'm not very tall, but I think I look OK. Mum says, "You look like your dad, Dale." My hair is dark like his. It's a bit long, but I'm not a prat.

I didn't talk to Mum about girls. I didn't talk to her much at all. She had all these boyfriends and I didn't have a girlfriend. I liked to think of her as a slag. It made me feel better.

I got fed up with school, so I didn't go any more. I kicked a ball around in the park or went to the chippie. My mate Kev stayed away from school, too. He was in a

gang. They stole cars and other stuff.

He asked me to be in his gang, but I said

no. So Kev called me a prat, same as

Sharon did. I didn't talk to him after that.

I didn't talk to anyone much.

A girl came to the park every day with a

little white dog. She had blond hair, longer

than mine, and she wore jeans and trainers

and a red top. I liked looking at her. She

smiled at me one day, and I smiled back.

We talked about her dog. He had long hair and a black nose. His name was Midge. The girl's name was Kate. I told her I was Dale. I told her I had a dog, but he got run over. His name was Jack. I wanted a new dog, but Mum said she was too busy. She had a job at the bingo hall, calling out the numbers. "On its own, number 9." All that stuff.

Kate said she went to bingo with her mum sometimes, but her mum was ill now. Kate was looking after her, so she didn't go to school. She didn't have a dad, same as me. Her dad left when Kate was a baby.

I liked Kate a lot, but I didn't ask her out. What if she said I was a prat? So we just sat on a seat in the park and talked. That was OK.

Then Mum met Greg.

He was a big man with a big car and a big smile. He had gold teeth, and he was a Pole. Mum said he was the man she had

been looking for. He wanted to look after her. She liked him a lot.

Greg wanted to look after me as well as Mum. He took me to football matches. I didn't want to go to football matches with Greg – he wasn't my dad. Other boys went with their dads, or with a girlfriend.

I wanted to ask Kate to come with me to a match. But I didn't ask her. I was sure she'd say no. I don't have any luck with girls. I would never be lucky.

Greg was lucky. He got a van when he came here from Poland. He rented it out, and soon he got another van. When Mum met him, he had 10 vans and a lot of men working for him. He didn't have much money to spend, but he said it didn't matter. He was doing well, renting out vans. He was happy.

Mum was happy, too. She left her job at the bingo hall. Now she was at home all day. She cleaned the house and made Greg fantastic meals. He got her a new cooker. He dug our bit of garden. On Sundays, he took Mum out in the car. He asked me to go, too, but I said no.

Greg and Mum were having a good time. I didn't want to be with them. I was on my own. I didn't want Greg to look after me, and I didn't want him to give me money. I wanted a job and money of my own. I wanted a dog. I wanted to be lucky. I wanted to win the Lottery. I wanted to be rich. I wanted Kate to be my girlfriend.

But I didn't have anything.

Chapter 2
Kev

One day I met Kev in the café. It was raining, and Kate wasn't in the park. I was feeling bad.

"Cheer up," Kev said.

"It's OK for you," I said. I told him about Kate and Greg and Mum.

Kev said, "You need money. Girls like a guy with money."

"Or they like a guy with luck," I said.

"Same thing," said Kev. "If you've got money, you're lucky. Tell you what – I can give you a job. Good money, cash in hand."

I said, "What sort of a job? Stealing cars?"

"No," said Kev. "You just put stuff in a van."

"When do you want me?" I asked. "And where do I go?"

"It's tonight," said Kev. "I'll show you where. You can come with me."

"OK," I said.

That night I met him at his place.
We got in his car. It was old, but it had
new paint. "New number plate, too," said
Kev. He laughed. So I knew he'd stolen it.

I asked, "Where are we going?"

He said, "You'll see."

We drove off. Kev stopped the car in a
dark car park behind a shop. He turned off
the lights.

"What do I have to do?" I asked.

"Put the stuff in the van," said Kev. "You'll see."

A van came into the car park. Its lights went off and a man got out. He opened the van's back doors.

Kev got out of the car, and so did I.

"Hi, Bob," Kev said to the man with the van. "Is Jim in the shop?"

"Yes," said Bob. "He got in by the window of the gents'. He's putting the stuff by the back door. The alarm-bell will ring when he opens the door, so we have to grab the stuff, quick."

We waited. It was cold. I began to shiver.

The shop door opened. The alarm-bell went off. It was very loud.

We ran to the door.

"Quick!" said Kev. "Get the stuff in the van."

He grabbed a box. I grabbed one, too.
It was hard to lift. I put it in the van. The
alarm-bell was still ringing.

"Get on with it," said Kev. "The cops will
be here in a moment."

I put in the next box. It was full of
bottles of booze.

I heard a police car. *Hee-hoo-hee-hoo* ...
I was at the shop door with a box.

Kev jumped in his car and started it.

"Wait!" I yelled. But he didn't wait.
He drove off.

Jim and Bob jumped into the van.

"Come on!" they yelled. "Quick!" But I
was too far away.

They drove out of the car park.
I dropped the box and ran after the van, but
it went too fast. It left me behind.

The police car was in the road. I was in its lights. Two cops jumped out and grabbed me.

They pushed me in the car.

Just wait till I see Kev, I thought. *I'll kill him.*

What could I say to the cops?

I was thinking hard, all the way to the police station.

Chapter 3
Cops

I told the cops it was nothing to do with me. I said I was walking down the road past the car park, when the shop alarm went off.

They asked why I was running out of the car park.

I said I saw a van in there, so I went to look. Then I got scared and ran.

The cops said I was one of the gang. They asked me for the names of the others. "I don't know," I said.

I kept on saying, "I don't know." It went on and on.

They asked my name and where I lived. Then they asked all over again. I kept telling them the same thing. I kept saying, "I'm not in the gang."

I knew they hadn't seen me with a box.
I knew I was OK. I just had to go on saying
I didn't know anything.

They let me phone Mum. She and Greg
came.

Mum yelled at me. She said I was
stupid. She said I mucked about at school
and never learned a thing and now I was
mucking up my life.

I said it was bad luck, but Mum went on yelling. She said everyone made their own luck, and she was fed up with me.

Greg said nothing. He drove us home in the car.

Mum said she was sorry. She made some tea. We sat down and talked.

Greg said Mum was right about making your own luck. His luck had been bad for years. He told me about it.

He used to drive a van in Poland. Then he was in a crash. He broke an arm and five ribs. His wife ran away with his best mate, and took his kids. His flat went on

fire and he lost everything. He got a new
job in a meat factory, but a dead pig fell on
him from a hook and broke his other arm.

Greg saved up some money to come to Britain. Then he got beaten up and robbed, so he lost it all. He saved up again, but the ticket cost all he had. When he came to Britain, he had nothing. But he started again.

"I'm OK now," he said. "I'm happy."

"Luck is funny stuff," Mum said. "It's good as well as bad. Never give up hope, Dale. One day, it will be good."

"Not for me," I said.

"Yes, it will," said Greg. "You'll see."

Chapter 4
Kate

The next day, I went to the café.

Kev was there. He was eating a burger.

"Sorry about last night," he said. "Did the cops get you?"

"Yes," I said.

"You didn't tell them our names?" he asked. He looked scared.

I said, "No, I didn't tell them."

"Great," said Kev. "You're a real mate. I'll buy you a Coke."

"Stuff your Coke," I said. I grabbed his burger, dropped it on the floor and trod on it. Then I went out.

I walked along the road to the park. Buses and cars went by. The sun was shining. I could still see Kev's face when I trod on his burger, and I felt great.

Kate was in the park. Her little dog, Midge, was running about. Kate was sitting on a seat. I sat on the seat as well.

I told her about last night.

I hoped she'd be nice about it, but she was as bad as Mum.

"You *are* stupid," she said. "The cops have your name now."

"But they let me go," I said.

"They let you go this time," said Kate, "but when the next shop gets done, they'll be looking for you."

I said, "It was just bad luck."

"It wasn't bad luck," said Kate. "It was stupid."

She got up and walked away.

She had her red top on. Her hair was very pale in the sun. I didn't want her to go.

I got up. "Kate!" I yelled. "Don't go!"

She didn't look back. She walked out of the park to the road. Midge was running in front of her.

Kate stopped on the kerb. She looked both ways.

Midge wasn't on the lead.

My dog Jack wasn't on the lead and he got run over. I ran after Kate.

"Look out!" I yelled.

Kate didn't look. She was at the traffic lights. They were going green and the cars and buses were starting up.

I tried to grab Midge, but he was too fast. He ran into the road, same as Jack did. I ran after him, into the traffic.

Brakes screeched. A van hit me. I was lying in the road. I had Midge in my arms. He was OK. Kate was screaming. All the traffic stopped.

I tried to stand up, but I couldn't. My leg hurt. So did my head.

A bus driver got out. He said to someone, "Get an ambulance!"

A man put a rug over me. I held on to Midge. He hadn't been run over. He was safe.

Kate was with me. She was crying. She took my hand in hers.

Then I blacked out.

Chapter 5
Luck

I woke up in the ambulance.

"Are you OK?" a man said.

"Fine," I said. My head hurt. I felt sick.

Kate was with me. She was holding Midge. She said, "I'm sorry, Dale. I was stupid."

I tried to say it was OK, but I blacked out again.

I had a broken leg and a cracked skull. My head was in a big bandage.

Mum and Greg came to see me in hospital.

"Why did you do it?" Mum asked.

I didn't know.

"It was the dog," I said. "Jack got killed."
It sounded stupid.

Mum looked as if she was going to cry.
She said, "I should have got you another
dog."

Greg said, "We'll get one when you come
home. To bring you luck."

Kate came to see me every day.

She said, "I'm sorry I said you were stupid. I was the stupid one. I got so cross, I forgot about Midge."

"It's OK," I said.

"Well, thanks anyway," Kate said. And she kissed me.

It all changed after that.

Greg and I went to the dogs' home and I got Bill. He's brown, and quite big.

He likes me a lot. And he gets on well with
Midge.

Kate is my girlfriend now. We both
leave school this summer. Her mum is

better, so Kate isn't looking after her now. She's going to be a hairdresser.

Greg is teaching me how to mend cars. I'm going to be a mechanic.

The police got Kev when he tried to rob a Post Office with a toy gun. An old lady hit him with her handbag, and he fell over her shopping trolley. Then a lot of people sat on him. What a prat!

I'm not a prat. I never was.

I never knew about luck, that's all.
I thought luck was things like winning the
Lottery, but it's not like that. Luck is
knowing how to be happy.

I know that now. I get bad days, but
most of the time, it's great.

I'm sorry I called Mum a slag. She was
just trying to change her luck. And she did.
My baby sister was born 3 weeks ago. She's
called Natasha, after Greg's mum.

My dog Bill thinks the baby is great.

Kate said we could have a baby, too, but I told her, no way.

I mean, we're happy, OK.

But don't push your luck.

Barrington Stoke would like to thank all its readers for commenting on the manuscript before publication and in particular:

E Armstrong

Simon Austin

Anthea Beale

Toby Bigge

Scott Ellis

Zoe Gale

Sara Gardner

Kash Green

Marguerite Hall

Corin Hancock

Kayleigh Lumsden

Martin McBride

Lisa Peck

Chris Young

Become a Consultant!

Would you like to give us feedback on our titles before they are published? Contact us at the address below – we'd love to hear from you!

Barrington Stoke, Sandeman House, Trunk's Close, 55 High Street, Edinburgh EH1 1SR
Tel: 0131 557 2020 Fax: 0131 557 6060
E-mail: info@barringtonstoke.co.uk
Website: www.barringtonstoke.co.uk

If you loved this book, why don't you read ...
Coma
by
David Belbin
ISBN 1-842991-97-3

GIRLFRIEND IN A COMA

A crash in the dark. Todd's girlfriend Lucy is in a coma. And now Todd's started seeing Jade. But what if Lucy wakes up ...?

You can order *Coma* directly from our website at
www.barringtonstoke.co.uk

If you loved this book,
why don't you read ...
The Beast
by
Michaela Morgan
ISBN 1-842991-98-1

BEAST IN THE WOODS

Oooooooooooooooo! Was it the
wind in the trees? Was it a ghost?
Or was it ... could it be ... a BEAST?

You can order *The Beast* directly from our
website at **www.barringtonstoke.co.uk**

If you loved this book, why don't you read ...

Torrent!

by

Bernard Ashley

ISBN 1-842991-96-5

RUN 4 YOUR LIFE!

Tod thinks he's going to die. The dam's broken. He's trapped.
He must get to the bridge before it's swept away! Who can save him now?

gr8reads